Everyone is Asleep But Me

By Diana Yacobi and Lily Safrani

Illustrated by Philip L. Wohlrab

Everyone is Asleep But Me
Copyright © 2018 by Diana Yacobi

Library of Congress Control Number:		2017958403
ISBN-13:	Paperback:	978-1-64151-242-8
	PDF:	978-1-64151-243-5
	ePub:	978-1-64151-244-2
	Kindle:	978-1-64151-245-9
	Hardcover:	978-1-64151-246-6

Printed in the United States of America

LitFire LLC
1-800-511-9787
www.litfirepublishing.com
order@litfirepublishing.com

Sleepy Bear opened his eyes.
It was dark and quiet
in his room.

*Sleepy Bear sat up
to look around.
Lion was sleeping.
His ball was sleeping.
His train was sleeping.
Was Mama Bear sleeping?*

He peeked into his
parents' room.
Was anyone awake?

The room was very quiet.
They were fast asleep.

Sleepy Bear was tired.
He wanted to lie down
but there was no room!
So he walked down the hall
and back to his room.

He looked around.
Lion was STILL sleeping.
His ball was STILL sleeping.
His train was STILL sleeping.
The SUN was STILL sleeping!

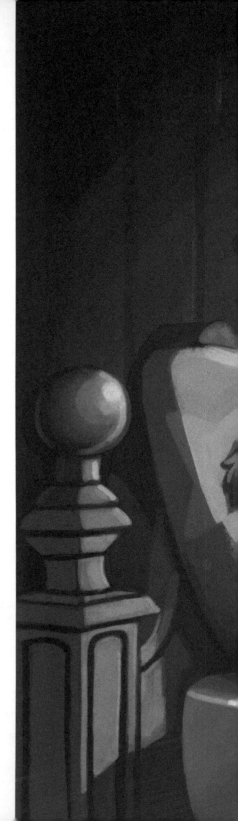

Sleepy Bear climbed
into the bed.
"Oh, it's warm and cozy."
Sleepy Bear closed his eyes
and fell asleep.

Night time is special.
Our body gets to rest in bed.
It's cozy and quiet.
And when the sun comes up
we have lots of energy
to play and start the new day.

Sleepy Bear is very proud.
He slept the WHOLE night in
his own bed!

So how did you sleep last night?
Put a mark on this chart
every time
you sleep the WHOLE night in
your own bed!